This **TW HOOTS** book
belongs to:

_____

First published in France 2015 by Editions Nathan Sejer
First published in the UK 2017 by Two Hoots
This edition published in the UK 2018 by Two Hoots
an imprint of Pan Macmillan
20 New Wharf Road, London N1 9RR
Associated companies throughout the world
www.panmacmillan.com
ISBN 978-1-5098-4272-8
Copyright © Editions Nathan Sejer, Paris – France 2015
Original edition: *Papa à Grands Pas*
English translation © Two Hoots 2017
Moral rights asserted.

9 8 7 6 5 4 3 2 1
A CIP catalogue record for this book is available from the British Library.
Printed in China
The illustrations in this book were created using Photoshop.

www.twohootsbooks.com

NADINE BRUN-COSME

DADDY
LONG
LEGS

AURÉLIE GUILLEREY

TW🦉 HOOTS

One morning, the old green car
had a lot of trouble starting.

It had the hiccups!

At last it got going, and Daddy drove Matty to nursery.

"See you later!" he said, giving
Matty a big kiss goodbye.

But Matty was worried.
"What if the car doesn't start again?" he said.
"You won't be able to pick me up."
Matty's dad thought for a bit.

Then he said,
"If the car doesn't start then I will
borrow the neighbour's big red tractor
and drive it over the fields to fetch you."

"But what if the big red tractor is too tired?" asked Matty.

"Then I will whistle to Martin, your lazy old teddy bear," his dad said. "He will lift me up with his giant paws and carry me to you on his back."

"But what if Martin is fast asleep and doesn't hear you?" asked Matty.

"Then I will go and round up all the birds in the garden," said his dad. "They will take me by the arms and fly me to you."

"But what if the birds are too busy looking after their babies?"

"Then I will call to the neighbour who waters his garden every day. He will turn up his hose and make a stream, and just like that I will jump into your little boat and sail straight to you."

"But what if the neighbour doesn't want to waste his water?" asked Matty.

"Then I will find the two rabbits who live at the end of the garden," said his dad. "I will put one under each foot, and they will hop me to you."

"But what if the rabbits have gone to see their granny?"

"Then I will call the big green dragon who breathes into the heater to keep us warm in winter," said Matty's dad. "And in two flaps of his wings and three big leaps, I will be right here with you!"

"But . . . what if the big dragon is out hunting?"
said Matty in a small voice.

"Ahhh," said Matty's dad.
"Well, if the tractor is too tired,
and Martin is fast asleep,
and the birds are busy taking care of their babies,
and the neighbour doesn't want to waste water,
and the rabbits are with their granny,
and the big dragon is out hunting . . ."

"Well then I will simply take to my own two feet and run. Because my legs will *never* be too tired to come and get you."

Nadine Brun-Cosme has been writing for children for over thirty years, creating picture books, graphic novels and plays. She has worked in schools, prisons and care homes – experiences which enrich her stories and her use of language.

Aurélie Guillerey was born in the beautiful city of Besançon, France. She illustrates stories at all hours in her loft, in Rennes, surrounded by a joyous mess. Her two boys, Clovis and Ambrose, regularly peek into her studio and often end up included in her books.